Korky
the
Mighty Elf

Linda Strachan
Illustrated by Mike Spoor

RIGBY

Korka was a very small elf.
He was smaller than all the other elves
on Elf Hill.

Korka always wanted to help the big elves.
"You are too small to help us," said one of
the big elves. "Just go home."

That night a **big**, **bad** troll came to Elf Hill.
The troll jumped on the elf houses
and squashed them.
The elves ran away into the wood.

Korka was in bed, asleep.
He was dreaming.
In his dream, he was
Korka the Mighty Knight,
saving his people from fright.

Suddenly Korka heard a **loud** crash.
He opened his eyes and saw a big troll foot.
Korka's bed was stuck on the troll's foot.

Then the troll ran back to his cave.
Korka jumped off the troll's foot.
"I'm glad the troll didn't see me,"
said Korka.

When the troll got back to the troll cave,
he boasted to the other trolls.
"I jumped on the elf houses and
I squashed them," he laughed.

"We want to do it, too!" said all the trolls.

Korka was hiding in the cave.

He heard what the trolls said.

"Oh, no!" said Korka. "I must stop the trolls."

Korka didn't know what to do.
Then he had an idea.
When the trolls were not looking,
he took some soap and a long pipe.

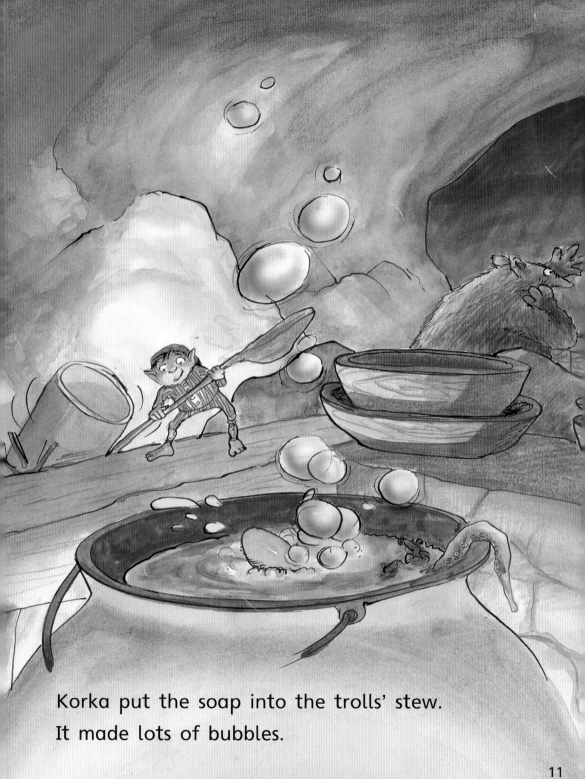

Korka put the soap into the trolls' stew.
It made lots of bubbles.

The trolls ate the stew.
It made them feel sick.
They **moaned** and they **groaned**,
and they had to lie down.

Korka stood in front of the fire.
His shadow was very tall.
Then he took the pipe and said,
"I am Korka the Mighty Elf."

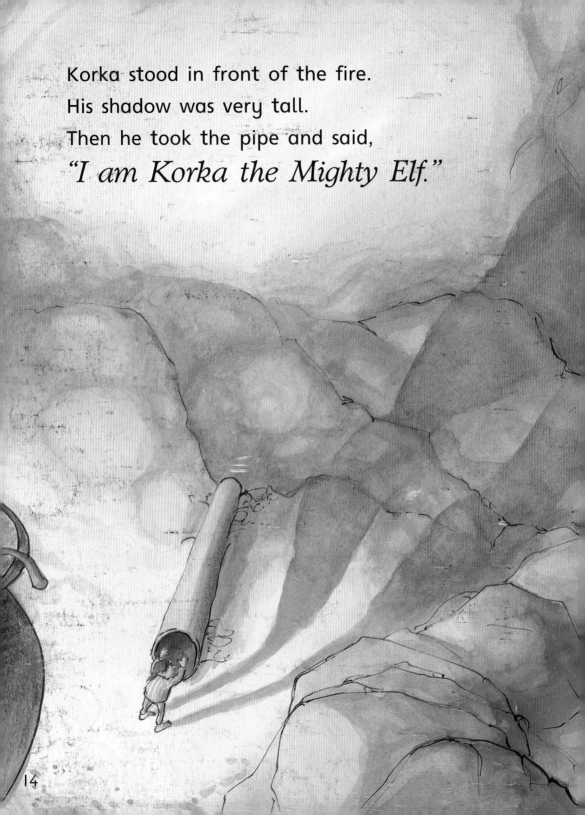

Korka's voice was very **LOUD**.
The trolls were very *scared*.
They screamed and they squealed,
and they all ran away.

The elves saw the trolls running away
and they came out of the wood.
The elves were proud of Korka.
"Thank you," they said.
"You may be the smallest elf, but
you are the *mightiest* elf of all."